HIS EXALTED EXCELLENCE

BRIAN IV
OF
JUTLAND

THE ROYAL POSTCARD COLLECTION

Ottoline and the Yellow Cat

Coming soon:

Ottoline Goes to School

Ottoline at Sea

Chris RIDDELL

Ottoline and the Yellow Cat

![HarperCollins] HarperCollins*Publishers*

For my daughter, Katy

Chapter One

Ottoline lived on the twenty-fourth floor of the Pepperpot Building. It was called the P. W. Huffledinck Tower; but it looked just like a pepper pot, so everyone called it the Pepperpot Building.

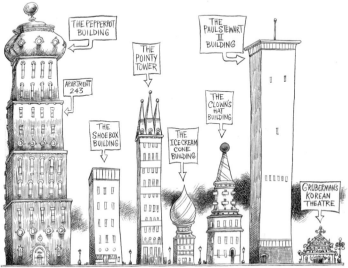

THE PEPPERPOT BUILDING

THE PAUL STEWART II BUILDING

THE POINTY TOWER

APARTMENT 243

THE CLOWN'S HAT BUILDING

THE SHOE BOX BUILDING

THE ICE CREAM CONE BUILDING

GRUBERMAN'S KOREAN THEATRE

LIKES SPLASHING IN PUDDLES AND COLLECTING THINGS

Ottoline

Mr. Munroe

SMALL, HAIRY, AND FROM A BOG IN NORWAY

She lived in apartment 243 with Mr. Munroe, who was small and hairy and didn't like the rain or having his hair brushed.

Ottoline, on the other hand, loved all kinds of weather, particularly rain, because she liked splashing in puddles. She also liked brushing Mr. Munroe's hair. She found it very relaxing, and it helped her to think, especially if there was a tricky problem to solve or a clever plan to work out.

Ottoline liked solving tricky problems and working out clever plans even more than she liked splashing in puddles. She kept her eyes and ears open in case she came across anything unusual or interesting. So did Mr. Munroe.

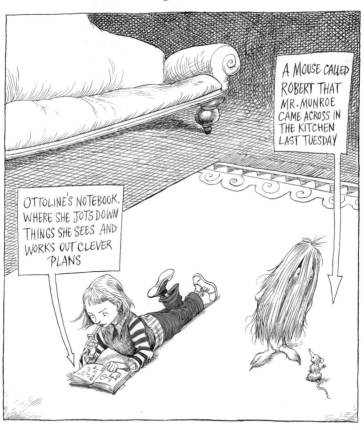

A MOUSE CALLED ROBERT THAT MR. MUNROE CAME ACROSS IN THE KITCHEN LAST TUESDAY

OTTOLINE'S NOTEBOOK, WHERE SHE JOTS DOWN THINGS SHE SEES AND WORKS OUT CLEVER PLANS

4 Ottoline's parents traveled the world collecting interesting things. Apartment 243 was full of the things that they collected.

EMPERORS' HATS

METEORITES

SEASHELLS

EXTREMELY SMALL PAINTINGS

SNUFF BOTTLES

HOT-WATER BOTTLES

BLUE BOTTLES

BUTTERFLY COLLECTORS' NETS

MASKS

PARROT CLOCKS

PORTABLE FISHBOWLS

LEAKING CUPS

Her parents had promised that one day, when she was older, Ottoline could join them on their travels, but until then she was to stay at home and look after their collections.

Ottoline didn't mind too much because she had Mr. Munroe for company.

MYSTERIOUS OBJECTS OF VARIOUS KINDS

One day, while out for an afternoon stroll, Mr. Munroe noticed a poster stuck to a lamppost outside Gruberman's Korean Theatre. He carefully peeled it off and folded it up. Then he put it under his arm, as, being small and hairy, Mr. Munroe didn't have any pockets. He took it home with him.

Puddle map

no cars allowed

Biggest splash here!

* Must remember to take the Bloomsbury double Umbrella

A PAGE FROM OTTOLINE'S NOTEBOOK

SLIGHTLY CHEWED BY ROBERT

Later that afternoon, Ottoline was dusting
the four-spouted teapot collection when she
felt a tap on her shoulder. It was Mr. Munroe.
He showed her the poster from the lamppost
outside Gruberman's Korean Theatre.

THE POSTER FROM THE LAMPPOST

lost

A Penangese lapdog
answers to the name
Rupert Pom-Pom Fluffy-Tail

Much missed by his loving owner

Large Reward

CONTACT: Mrs. Loretta Lloyd, Apartment 11112,
The Pointy Tower, 3rd st., B.C.

ARMPIT HAIR

"How interesting," Ottoline said. "You don't
have any more of these by any chance?"

Mr. Munroe went to his room. It was very untidy.

When he came back, Ottoline was reorganizing her Odd Shoe collection.

Ottoline had two collections that were all her own. One was her Odd Shoe collection, of which she was very proud. Whenever Ottoline bought a pair of shoes, she would wear one and put the other in her collection.

IF YOU'D LIKE TO FIND OUT ABOUT OTTOLINE'S OTHER COLLECTION, TURN TO PAGE 45.

SOME OF OTTOLINE'S ODD SHOES

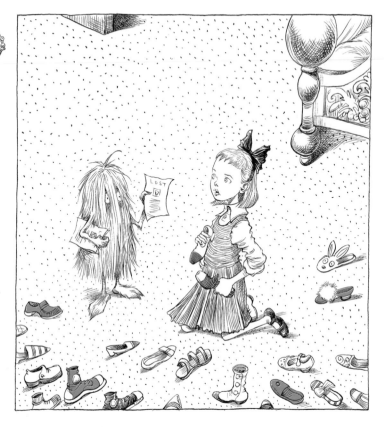

Mr. Munroe showed Ottoline the posters he'd
collected from lampposts all over town.

Ottoline looked at them for a long time.
"I don't suppose . . . ," she said, "you'd let me
brush your hair?"

While she brushed Mr. Munroe's hair,
Ottoline looked more closely at the posters.

THIS IS WHAT OTTOLINE LOOKS LIKE WHEN SHE'S THINKING OF A CLEVER PLAN.

WILSON
HAPPY-EARS
McMURTAGH

COUNT OLTO
VIX-HILBURG

FIFI FIESTA
FUNNY-FACE
III

That evening Ottoline and Mr. Munroe sat
down to dinner. Ottoline had grilled cheese and
cinnamon toast freshly delivered to the table by

Marion's
Bathroom
Supplies

Smith &
Smith
PILLOW-PLUMPING &
CURTAIN-DRAWING
TECHNICIANS

The
Smiling
Dragon
CLOTHES-FOLDING
Cº.

THE
1,000-STRONG
LIGHTBULB-CHANGING
Cº.

The Home-Cooked Meal Co. Mr. Munroe
had a bowl of porridge and a mug of hot
chocolate, which was the only meal he ever ate.

Happy Nest
BED MAKERS

THE
Home-Cooked
Meal Co.

Mr.
Munroe

OTTOLINE'S
PARENTS WERE
AWAY A LOT
TRAVELING, BUT
THEY MADE SURE
OTTOLINE
WAS WELL
LOOKED AFTER
BY LOTS AND
LOTS OF PEOPLE.
THESE ARE
THEIR BUSINESS
CARDS.

D.H.S.
DOOR HANDLE
SHINERS
INC.

MB
McBEAN'S CLEANING
SERVICE

After dinner Ottoline went down to the laundry room in the basement of the Pepperpot Building.

Ottoline liked to do her own laundry for two reasons. Firstly, she liked the washing machines . . .

BILL   BEN

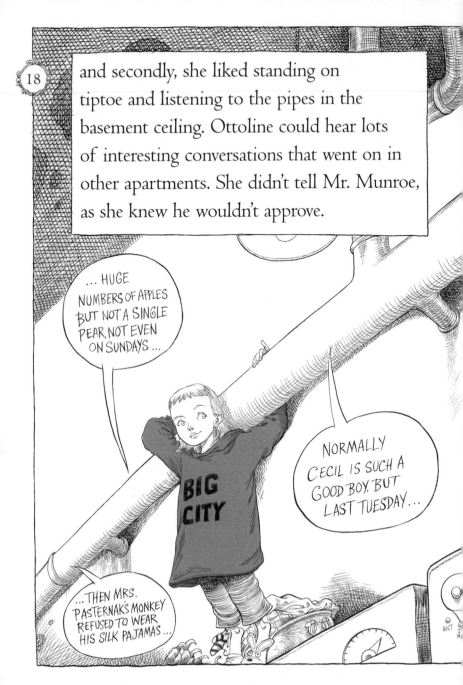

and secondly, she liked standing on tiptoe and listening to the pipes in the basement ceiling. Ottoline could hear lots of interesting conversations that went on in other apartments. She didn't tell Mr. Munroe, as she knew he wouldn't approve.

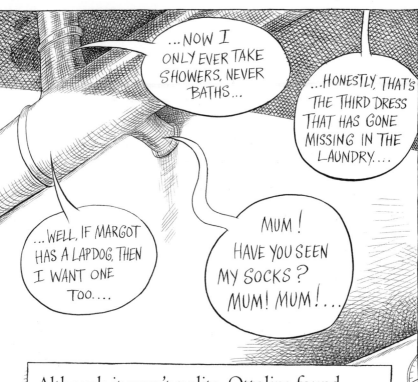

Although it wasn't polite, Ottoline found eavesdropping often helped her to solve tricky problems and think of clever plans.

It was Ottoline who found Mrs. Pasternak's missing monkey with a trail of honey-coated peanuts. And when the man from apartment 36 got his toe stuck in a tap, it was Ottoline who called the fire department.

That evening, Ottoline was doing her laundry
and listening to the pipes as usual when
a large, hairy arm appeared from behind
one of the washing machines and grabbed
a pair of Ottoline's stripy socks.

Ottoline peered into the shadows.

It was a bear.

"You ought to be ashamed of
yourself, stealing socks," said
Ottoline.

"So should you, listening
in on other people's
conversations," said
the bear.

"I won't tell
if you won't,"
said Ottoline.

Chapter Two

ROBERT IS IN THE HABIT OF READING OVER PEOPLE'S SHOULDERS.

MR. MUNROE IS IN THE HABIT OF DROPPING THE PAGES HE'S NOT INTERESTED IN ON THE FLOOR.

Mr. Munroe was sitting in the Beidermeyer armchair, reading the newspaper. Mr. Munroe often read his newspaper if he had trouble getting to sleep or had a bad dream about the bog in Norway. He liked to read the travel section, about vacations on tropical islands and sunny beaches.

Several pages caught Ottoline's eye.

Ottoline got out a pair of Balinese pinking shears from the scissors collection and carefully cut out the articles. Mr. Munroe didn't notice. He was engrossed in a story about the Gobi Desert, where it hardly ever rains.

IF YOU WOULD LIKE TO SEE THIS PAGE OF OTTOLINE'S NOTEBOOK, TURN THE PAGE.

NO NEW LEADS IN SHOE BOX BUILDING BURGLARY

By our crime correspondent

Police remain baffled by the burglary in the Shoe Box Building on 3rd Street. Despite extensive inquiries and prolonged investigations, Police Commissioner Ronald Flatfoot admitted, "We remain baffled." The victim of the burglary, Mrs. Rachel Armstrong, was too upset to talk to the *Enquirer* last night but said in a written statement, "I have nothing further to add." Police appealed to the public to be vigilant and on their guard at all times.

Mrs. Rachel Armstrong

*These dogs look strangely familiar

Mr. Munroe with a haircut!

BURGLARY AT THE POINTY TOWER BAFFLES POLICE

By our crime correspondent

Police remain baffled by the burglary at the Pointy Tower on Third Street. Despite extensive inquiries and prolonged investigations, Police Commissioner Ronald Flatfoot admitted, "We remain baffled." The victim of the burglary, Mrs. Dominica Wilson, was too outraged to talk to the *Enquirer* last night but said in a written statement, "I'm too outraged to talk." Police appealed to the public to be vigilant and on their guard at all times.

Mrs. Dominica Wilson

ANOTHER BURGLARY ON 3RD STREET LEAVES NO CLUES

By our crime correspondent

Mrs. Pinky Neugerbauer

Police were baffled last night by another burglary on Third Street. In an audacious cat burglary on an apartment on the fifteenth floor of the Ice-Cream Cone Building, jewelry worth quite a lot was stolen. Despite initial inquiries and prolonged investigations, Police Commissioner Ronald Flatfoot admitted, "We are baffled." The victim of the burglary, Mrs. Pinky Neugerbauer, was too shocked to talk to the *Enquirer* last night but said in a written statement, "I'm in shock." Police appealed to the public to be vigilant and on their guard at all times.

* Must investigate this ←

I wonder what has been nibbling my notebook? ↘

That night, after the Smith & Smith technicians had plumped the pillows and drawn the curtains, Ottoline got out of bed and went to her Special Disguises Wardrobe. Ottoline was a Mistress of Disguise and had a diploma to prove it, from the Who-R-U Academy of Subterfuge.

THIS IS THE DIPLOMA.

ACADEMY OF SUBTERFUGE

THIS IS TO CERTIFY THAT

Ottoline Brown

IS A CERTIFIED MISTRESS OF DISGUISE

PROFESSOR MYSTERY M.D.

When she was ready, she knocked on
Mr. Munroe's door.

"Your hair could do with a brush," said
Ottoline when he opened the door, "but we
haven't got time for that now. Here, put this
on." She handed Mr. Munroe a large, shabby
raincoat.

Mr. Munroe
handed her an
umbrella just
in case.

They set off through the city.

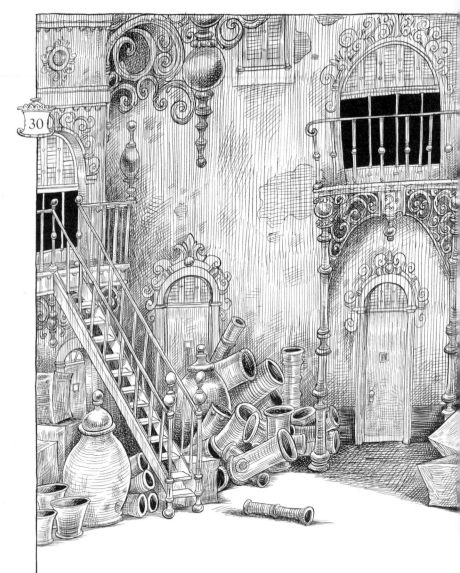

And very soon were . . .

They came to an old warehouse.

Ottoline studied her notebook.

There was a sign on the door that read:

Mr. Munroe was going to ring the bell,
but Ottoline stopped him. Instead they
looked through a rather grubby window.
This is what they saw. . . .

The poker players looked strangely familiar. Behind them, a cockatoo was talking into a telephone.

"I'm very sorry, madam, but that's company policy," the cockatoo was saying. "If you lose a lapdog we supplied you with, we can't trust you with another one, now can we? Good-bye."

The cockatoo put down the receiver.

Just then a yellow cat walked in.

"Good evening, boys," she purred. "Had a good week?"

The poker players wagged their tails.

"Excellent," purred the Yellow Cat. "Given Mrs. Neugerbauer the slip, I see, McMurtagh," she said, patting a small Lancashire terrier on the head.

"That's right, Boss," snarled the dog. "I ran out of the poodle parlor after one of those perfumed baths, and kept on running."

"Good work," said the Yellow Cat. "Now, boys, time for business. Show me what you've got."

The poker players put down their cards and picked up their pencils and started scribbling.

"Bring them to me, Clive!" said the Yellow Cat.

The cockatoo flapped about gathering up the drawings in his beak and took them to the Yellow Cat.

"Excellent," she purred.

THIS IS ONE OF THEM

my bed

Kitshun

Open Window

bed room

sitting room

Front door

Jewels

2880, Clown's hat Bilding

A Penangese lapdog dropped his doggy
chew. "I ran off in the park this morning.
Mrs. Lloyd threw me a stick, and she's still
waiting for it. But I'm not going back!"

The Yellow Cat smiled. "If this
information is correct, my furry
friend," she purred, "then
you won't have to!"

Chapter Three

The next morning Ottoline woke up rather later than usual. She put on her Mongolian dressing gown and, stifling a yawn, shuffled down the hallway.

There was a postcard on the doormat.

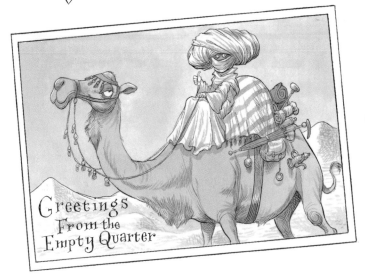

Greetings
From the
Empty Quarter

43

Dearest O, on the trail
of the most spectacular
camel hair coat to add
to our collection. Please
try not to spill jam down
the front of your mongolian
dressing gown, there's a dear.
The desert is very hot and it
never rains here. Mr. Munroe would
love it! Pa sends his love,
                            Ma
P.S. Remember to put the umbrella
back in the stand and don't
stay up too late tonight!
                    x x x

POSTCARD

EMPTY
E 4·02·07
QUARTE

Miss O. Brown,
Apt. 243,
The Pepperpot Bld.
3rd Street,
BIG CITY 3001

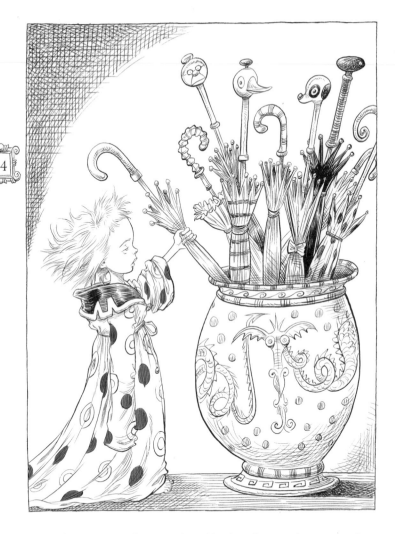

Ottoline put the umbrella back in the stand
and yawned sleepily.

Then she went to her room to put the postcard in her Postcard collection.

Ottoline loved her Postcard collection even more than her Odd Shoe collection. This was because all the postcards were from her parents.

Ottoline liked looking at the pictures of faraway places on the fronts of the postcards . . .

THIS IS OTTOLINE'S SECOND COLLECTION.

. . . and she loved reading the messages on the backs, because they made her feel as if her parents weren't so far away.

These are a few of her favorites:

Greetings From the Far East

Greetings From the Frozen South

IF YOU WANT TO READ THE MESSAGES ON THE BACK, TURN THE PAGE. →

POSTCARD

Dearest O, Have never seen so many polar bears! The igloo we are staying in is very warm and snug. Please remember to shut the fridge door, there's a love. It's snowing again; don't think Mr. Munroe would like it here. Pa sends his love,
Ma
P.S. On your walks, make sure Mr. Munroe wraps up warm in Pa's raincoat. XXX

FROZEN NORTH
13·04·05

6248¢

Miss O. Brown,
Apt. 243,
The Pepperpot Bld.
3rd Street,
BIG CITY 3001

POSTCARD

Dearest O, Finally we have found the Emperor of Heligoland's walking hat! Pa sends his love, lots of love,
Ma
P.S. Put the top back on the toothpaste!
X X X

WILD WEST
10·06·06
4¢

Miss O. Brown,
Apt. 243,
The Pepperpot Bld.
3rd Street,
BIG CITY 3001

POSTCARD

Dearest O, ran across some butterfly collectors in the jungle here. Pa was VERY CROSS and took away their butterfly collectors' nets! He sends his love,
Ma
P.S. Tidy your Odd Shoe collection, there's a good girl! xxx

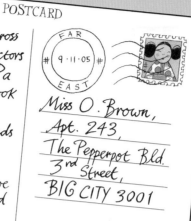

Miss O. Brown,
Apt. 243,
The Pepperpot Bld.
3rd Street,
BIG CITY 3001

POSTCARD

Dearest O, There are penguins everywhere! Emperor penguins, King Penguins and Vice-President penguins... The ship is frozen solid in the ice so we're stuck here for a bit. Don't forget to dust the four-spouted teapot collection, my darling, Pa sends his love,
Ma
P.S. Well done! A diploma in disguise is a very useful thing to have.

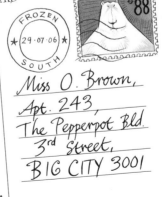

Miss O. Brown,
Apt. 243,
The Pepperpot Bld.
3rd Street,
BIG CITY 3001

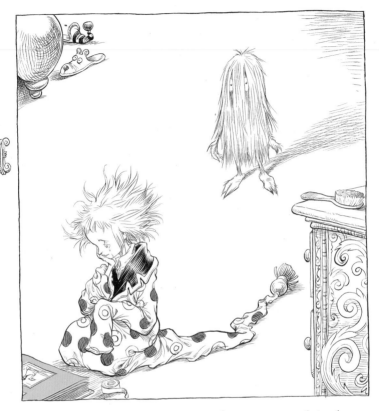

Ottoline was just putting the postcard in her collection when Mr. Munroe walked in. She showed him the postcard.

He looked at it for a long time and then picked up Ottoline's hairbrush.

"My hair needs brushing?" asked Ottoline.

Mr. Munroe nodded. Next to having his own
hair brushed, the thing he liked least was
brushing someone else's. But he knew that it
would make Ottoline feel better, so he did
the best he could.

For breakfast that morning Ottoline
had strawberry bagels and apple juice.
Mr. Munroe had porridge and hot chocolate,

which he didn't touch because he was too
busy reading the newspaper.

"It's rude to read at the table," said Ottoline.

After breakfast, as they sat together on the Beidermeyer sofa, Mr. Munroe showed Ottoline something he had underlined in the newspaper in red crayon.

ROBERT FINISHED MR. MUNROE'S PORRIDGE FOR HIM, WHICH MADE HIM FEEL RATHER FULL

55

OTTOLINE LIKED TO CHANGE HER HAIRSTYLE EVERY DAY. ON TUESDAYS SHE GENERALLY WORE BRAIDS AND A BOW.

MR. MUNROE'S HAIRSTYLE NEVER CHANGED.

TO SEE WHAT MR. MUNROE UNDERLINED, TURN THE PAGE.

THE BIG CITY ENQUIRER

CAT BURGLAR STRIKES AGAIN

By our crime correspondent

Mrs. Loretta Lloyd

Mrs. Loretta Lloyd of the Clown's Hat Building on Third Street was the latest victim to fall prey to the "Notorious Cat Burglar." Mrs. Lloyd lost jewelry worth quite a lot in the robbery and was too angry to talk to the *Enquirer* last night but said in a written statement, "I'm so angry!" Police Commissioner Ronald Flatfoot admitted, "We are baffled," and appealed to the public to be vigilant and on their guard at all times.

"Mr. Munroe," said Ottoline, "I think it's time you practiced your Special Disguises."

Chapter Four

Just then the doorbell rang. Mr. Munroe went to the front door and opened it.

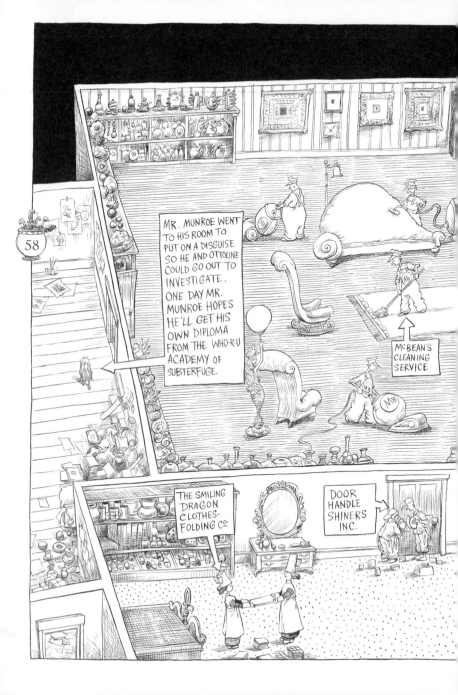

MR. MUNROE WENT TO HIS ROOM TO PUT ON A DISGUISE SO HE AND OTTOLINE COULD GO OUT TO INVESTIGATE.

ONE DAY MR. MUNROE HOPES HE'LL GET HIS OWN DIPLOMA FROM THE WHO-R-U ACADEMY OF SUBTERFUGE.

McBEAN'S CLEANING SERVICE

THE SMILING DRAGON CLOTHES-FOLDING CO.

DOOR HANDLE SHINERS INC.

58

1,000-STRONG
LIGHT-BULB-
CHANGING
Cᵒ.

OTTOLINE
LIKED TO
SUPERVISE

THE HOME-
COOKED
MEAL Cᵒ.

59

SMITH & SMITH
PILLOW-PLUMPING
AND CURTAIN-DRAWING
TECHNICIANS

MARION'S
BATHROOM
SUPPLIES

HAPPY NEST
BED
MAKERS

AT TEN O'CLOCK Mr. Munroe came out of his room and tapped Ottoline on the shoulder. He was wearing a large, shabby raincoat.

Ottoline checked the curtains.

"Not now, Mr. Munroe," she said.

Mr. Munroe went back to his room.

AT ELEVEN O'CLOCK Mr. Munroe tapped
Ottoline on the shoulder again. He was
wearing a large, shabby raincoat and a pair
of dark glasses.

Ottoline looked at the door handle.

"Not now, Mr. Munroe," she said.

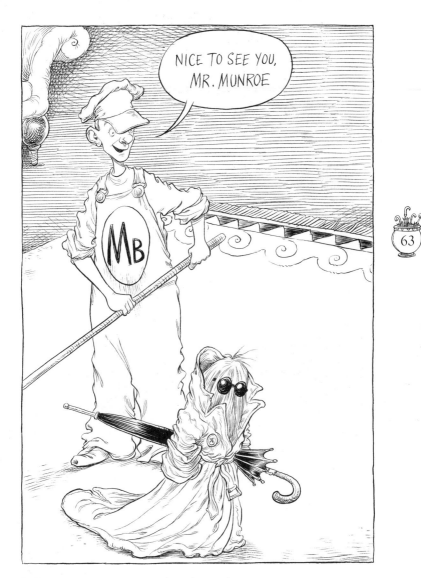

Mr. Munroe went back to his room.

AT TWELVE O'CLOCK Mr. Munroe coughed loudly. He was wearing a large, shabby raincoat, a pair of dark glasses and the Emperor of Heligoland's hat.

Ottoline examined the toothpaste.

"Not now, Mr. Munroe," she said.

Mr. Munroe went back to his room and
slammed the door.

MR. MUNROE!

At lunch . . .

. . . there was very little conversation.

Mr. Munroe was wearing a large shabby rain-coat, a pair of dark glasses, the Emperor of Heligoland's hat and an extremely long scarf.

AT THREE O'CLOCK

Ottoline inspected her knickers.

"Not now," she said.

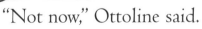

AT FOUR O'CLOCK

"Not now," Ottoline said.

AT FIVE O'CLOCK

"Not now."

73

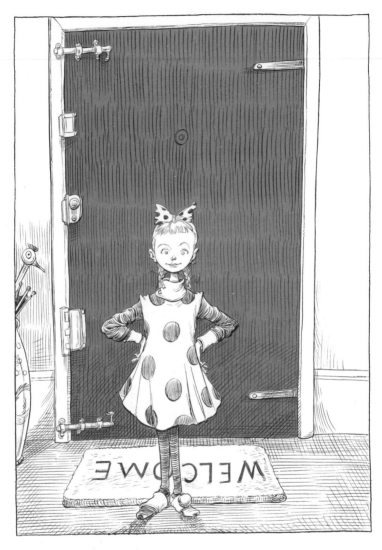

When everyone had gone, Ottoline closed the
front door and turned around.

"Now, Mr. Munroe," she said, "what is it . . . ?"

But Mr. Munroe wasn't there.

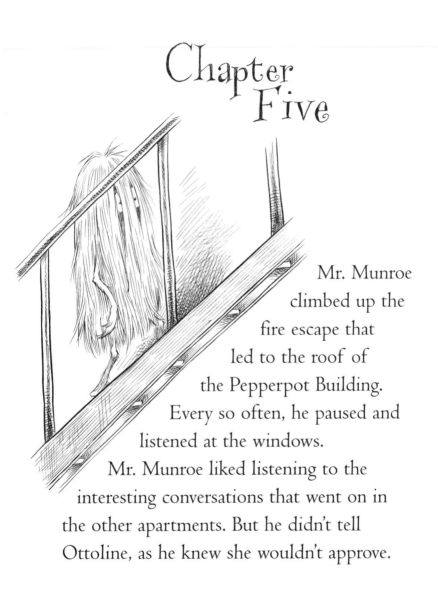

Chapter Five

Mr. Munroe
climbed up the
fire escape that
led to the roof of
the Pepperpot Building.
Every so often, he paused and
listened at the windows.
Mr. Munroe liked listening to the
interesting conversations that went on in
the other apartments. But he didn't tell
Ottoline, as he knew she wouldn't approve.

Mr. Munroe stood on the roof of the Pepperpot Building and thought for a long time.

It began to rain ...

81

. . . very heavily.

82

As he stood in the rain, Mr. Munroe thought about the cold, wet bog in Norway. He remembered how Ottoline's parents, Professor and Professor Brown, had found him and had invited him to come home with them to the Pepperpot Building.

Professor Brown lent him his nice new raincoat, and Professor Brown gave him her sunglasses. The three of them sailed home on the SS *Trondheim*. To avoid unwanted attention they called him Mr. Munroe, although his real name was something in Norwegian that meant "Small-Hairy-Bog-Person."

85

From the
moment she
was born,
Ottoline and
Mr. Munroe were
inseparable.

He took her for walks.

He let her brush his hair.

He even let her give him a bath . . .

. . . but only once.

But whatever they did, Ottoline's parents
knew that as long as Mr. Munroe was with
her, their daughter would always be safe.

The rain stopped, and Mr. Munroe went
down the fire escape. He didn't feel sad
any longer.

He stood on the doormat until he had
stopped dripping.

It felt good to be out of the rain. It felt
good to be far away from the bog in Norway.
It felt good to be living in
the Pepperpot
Building.

Most of all, it felt good to have Ottoline as
his best friend.

Mr. Munroe found Ottoline sitting in the
Beidermeyer
rocking
chair.

OTTOLINE
WAS MAKING
NOTES IN HER
NOTEBOOK.

MR. MUNROE
KNEW HOW
RELAXING OTTOLINE
FOUND BRUSHING
HIS HAIR,
ESPECIALLY AFTER
A BUSY DAY.

92

"Would you like me to brush your hair?"
asked Ottoline.

Mr. Munroe nodded.

When she had finished, Ottoline looked at
Mr. Munroe for a long time. Then she looked
at her notebook.

"I've got a clever plan," she said.

Chapter
Six

Late that night, there was a knock on the door of the old warehouse.

"Go away!" yelled the Yellow Cat. "We're closed! Callers by appointment only!"

There was another knock on the door, followed by a rather feeble bark.

"All right, all right," complained the Yellow Cat. "Keep your tail on. I'm coming, I'm coming!"

The Yellow Cat opened the door. There was a small, hairy dog outside. The small, hairy dog handed the Yellow Cat a card.

THIS IS WHAT THE CARD READ.

Bimby Bottlenose II
Emperor of Heligoland
Pedigree Norwegian Lapdog

95

"Lapdog, eh?" said the Yellow Cat. "Then you've come to the right place!" She stepped aside and let him in.

"Look what the cat dragged in," said the Yellow Cat. "Boys, meet Bimby Bottlenose, Emperor of Heligoland."

The poker players looked up from their game.

"We can call him Nosy," said the Yellow Cat. "Nosy, meet the gang."

RUPE THE FANG

SNARLER McMURTAGH

BUTCH HILBURG

THE SUNDANCE PUP

The gang wagged their tails and made room
for Nosy at the table.

"Clive!" said the Yellow Cat. "Make sure the
boys don't stay up too late. We've got work
tomorrow."

"You're the boss, Boss," squawked the
cockatoo.

"So where are you
from, stranger?" said
Rupe the Fang.
Nosy gave him his card.
Rupe looked at it.
"Norway," he said.
"It can get very wet
in Norway."
Nosy nodded and put a
playing card on the table.

"Emperor of Heligoland?"
said Butch Hilburg, chewing
on his doggy treat. "I once
saw the Emperor of
Heligoland. Wore a
splendid hat."

Nosy nodded
and played
another card.

"Care for a doggy treat?" offered McMurtagh.

Nosy shook his head.

"Don't say much, do you?" McMurtagh snarled. "What's wrong? Cat got your tongue?"

"Don't mind him," said The Sundance Pup. "He's just sore because his last owner took him to the poodle parlor for a shampoo."

Nosy laid his playing cards on the table.

"Full house!" squawked Clive. "You win! Time for bed!"

Nosy didn't sleep well in the lapdogs'
basket. Rupe the Fang snored, Snarler
McMurtagh whimpered, Butch Hilburg
chased squirrels in his dreams, and The
Sundance Pup
had terrible
gas.

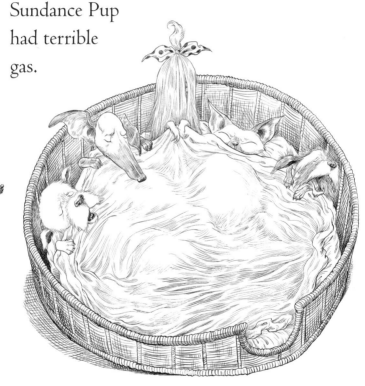

He was just beginning to doze off when the
door opened and the Yellow Cat crept in.

The Yellow Cat opened her bag and took out an emerald necklace, which she carefully hid beneath the floorboards.

Just then, the telephone rang. The Yellow Cat leaped in the air with surprise, and Clive woke up with a squawk. "Don't just perch there!" hissed the Yellow Cat. "Answer it."

Clive picked up the receiver.

"The Lapdog Agency, how may we help you?" he said. "A lapdog? Certainly, madam. We have an excellent selection. Would you care to make an appointment . . . this morning? . . . Yes, I think we can fit you in. . . . What time? . . . Now? Well, I suppose . . . Let me see. . . ."

Just then there was a knock at the door.

"Must I do EVERYTHING myself?" said the Yellow Cat, slinking up the stairs.

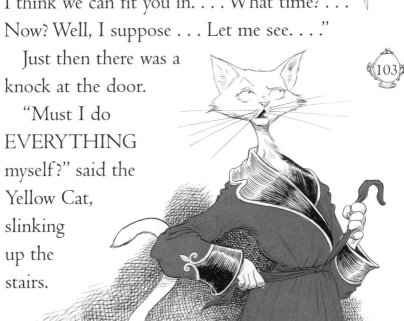

Chapter Seven

The Yellow Cat opened the door. An extremely large lady was standing on the doorstep.

"Can I help you?" said the Yellow Cat.

"Mrs. Ursula Jansen-Smith," said the large lady grandly. "I am an incredibly rich but lonely old lady, and I'd like a lapdog to take home with me. I've just made an appointment."

Clive put down the telephone.

"Please come in, Mrs. Jansen-Smith," purred the Yellow Cat.

"You can call me Ursula," said the lady.

THE LAMPSHADE FROM PAGE 14

THE EXTREMELY LONG SCARF FROM PAGE 68

THE SUNGLASSES FROM PAGE 85

THE FUR COAT FROM PAGE 20

THE GLOVES FROM PAGE 70

"Showtime!" said the Yellow Cat.

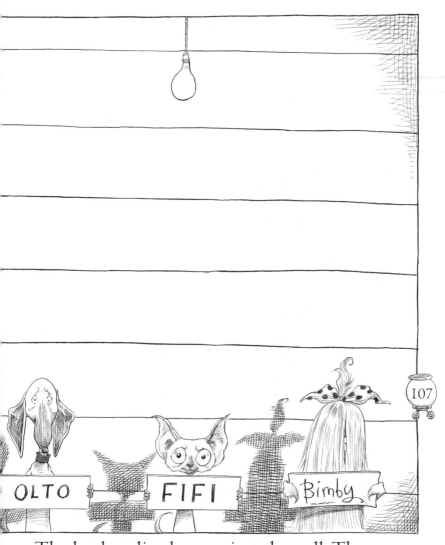

The lapdogs lined up against the wall. They
held cards with their lapdog names on them.

Mrs. Jansen-Smith walked slowly down the line and looked carefully at each lapdog.

108

"Can I just say what an exquisite hat you're wearing, Mrs. Jansen-Smith?" purred the Yellow Cat, rubbing her paws. "And what a simply stunning outfit."

109

"My hat?" said Mrs. Jansen-Smith. "Do you like it? It was a present from the Emperor of Jutland. And these things? Oh, they're straight from the laundry. I just threw them together!"

Mrs. Jansen-Smith stopped in front of the last lapdog.

"I'll take this one," she said.

"Excellent choice," purred the Yellow Cat. "Bimby Bottlenose, Emperor of Heligoland, is a pedigree Norwegian lapdog."

"It can get very wet in Norway," said Mrs. Jansen-Smith thoughtfully. "Send me the bill. Apartment 243, the Pepperpot Building, Third Street."

When Mr. Munroe got back to apartment 243, he found a postcard on the doormat. He picked it up and went to see Ottoline. She was busy writing in her notebook.

Mr. Munroe handed her the postcard.

"Your ribbon has come undone," she said.

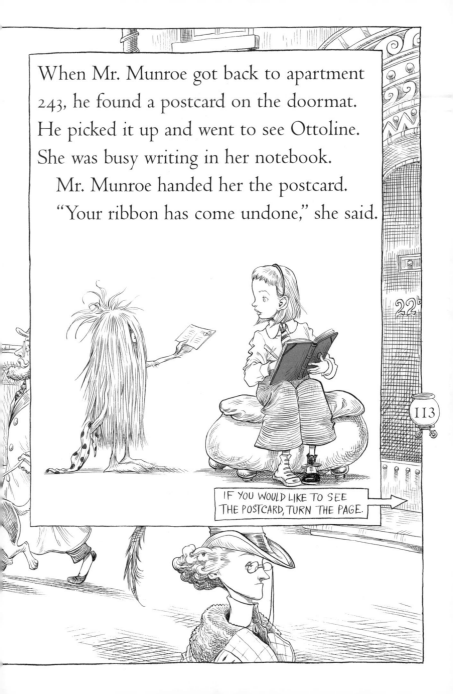

IF YOU WOULD LIKE TO SEE THE POSTCARD, TURN THE PAGE.

113

POSTCARD

Dearest O',

Pa has found some splendid new umbrellas.

Lots of love,
Ma

P.S. Make sure Mr. Munroe gets to bed!
X X X

TRONDHEIM
NORWAY
B. 28.4.07

Miss O. Brown,
Apt. 243,
The Pepperpot Building
3rd Street,
BIG CITY 3001

115

"It looks very wet, doesn't it, Mr. Munroe,"
said Ottoline. "Mr. Munroe . . . ?"

But Mr. Munroe was fast asleep.

Chapter Eight

The next morning, Mr. Munroe got up bright and early. He wandered around the apartment . . .

. . . making careful notes.

243

OTTOLINE'S
BOLIVIAN LLAMA-
WOOL ROBE →

HOME · COOKED
CUSTARD PIE
HOME · COOKED
CUSTARD PIE
HOME · COOKED
CUSTARD PIE

The doorbell rang. Ottoline went to the front
door and opened it.

"We're not too early, I hope," said the chef from The Home-Cooked Meal Company.

"No," said Ottoline. "There's lots to get ready."

For breakfast, Ottoline had waffles and maple syrup. Mr. Munroe had porridge and hot chocolate, which he didn't touch because he was busy finishing his notes.

"It's rude to write at the table," said
Ottoline.

After breakfast, as they sat on the Beidermeyer ottoman, Mr. Munroe showed Ottoline his notes.

She looked at them for a long time and then she said, "Good work, Mr. Munroe."

ROBERT CARRYING A PIECE OF LEFTOVER WAFFLE

Then Ottoline brushed Mr. Munroe's hair . . .

. . . very
thoroughly . . .

. . . and tied a ribbon in it.

She kissed him on the forehead.

"You're very brave," she said. "Now you'd better go."

Mr. Munroe nodded.

Ottoline waited until Mr. Munroe had gone, and then she walked to Gruberman's Korean Theatre. She carefully unfolded a poster and stuck it to the lamppost.

LOST

A Pedigree Norwegian
Lapdog
answers to the name of
Bimby Bottlenose II
Emperor of Heligoland
Much missed by his loving owner
LARGE REWARD
Contact Mrs. Jansen-Smith Apartment 243
THE PEPPERPOT BUILDING · 3rd street · B.C.

129

Mr. Munroe knocked on the warehouse door.

"Hiya, Nosy," the Yellow Cat said. "You're a fast worker."

REPAIRED
BUTTERFLY
COLLECTOR'S
NET

133

IF YOU WOULD LIKE TO SEE THE PIECE OF PAPER, TURN THE PAGE.

The gang crowded round.

"OK, show me what you've got," said the Yellow Cat.

Nosy handed her a piece of paper.

Apartment 243, the Pepperpot Building

Emperors' hats

extremely
small paintings

sofa

NOTHING
interesting
HERE!

rocking
Chair

Collections

armchair

134

odd shoe
collection

dressing table

Wardrobe

Fire
Escape

Window

Mrs.
Jansen-Smith's
Bedroom

Window

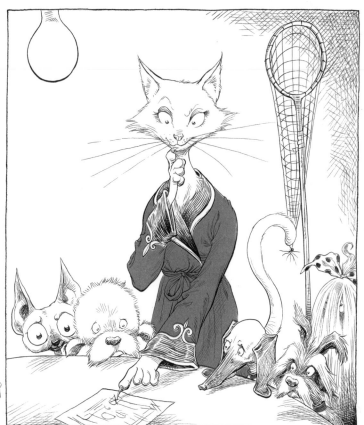

The Yellow Cat looked at the drawing for a long time. "Excellent work, Nosy," she purred as she left the room. "Excellent."

"Welcome back," snarled Snarler McMurtagh. "Feeling lucky?"

Nosy nodded and sat down at the table with the other lapdogs. Butch Hilburg dealt the cards.

"Didn't take you long to give your owner the slip," said Rupe the Fang. "Very careless, some of these ladies."

Nosy nodded again and played a card.

"So is the rumor true?" Butch said to Rupe. "Are you thinking of going back to Mrs. Lloyd?"

"What if I am?" replied Rupe. "Sometimes a dog just wants a quiet lap to sit on for the rest of his days. I'm getting too old for a life on the run."

"I miss Mrs. Armstrong," said The Sundance Pup with a sniff.

Nosy put his last card on the table.

"Full house!" squawked Clive the cockatoo. "You win!"

Chapter Nine

That night, as the lapdogs slept in their basket, the Yellow Cat tiptoed up the stairs and out of the door without a sound.

Butch Hilburg turned over and thumped his tail, and Rupe the Fang licked his chops noisily and got comfortable before he started snoring again.

Mr. Munroe
gently
removed
Snarler
McMurtagh's
front paws from
his head and
quietly climbed
out of the basket.

Reaching up, he tugged his
bow undone and let the ribbon fall to
the floor. Then he tiptoed across to the
corner of the room.

Mr. Munroe carefully
tilted the loose floor-
board. It gave a
small creak.

Clive woke up and saw Mr. Munroe with the loot. He let out a piercing screech: "Stop, thief!"

But Mr. Munroe was prepared.

He tied up Clive firmly with the polka-dot
ribbon, wrapping it once around his legs,
twice around his wings, and three times
around his beak. He then tied a bow in it and
pulled it tight.

"Umph! Umph! Umph!" said Clive.

Mr. Munroe then sat down at the table,
picked up the telephone, and started to dial. . . .

Just then the doorbell rang, and the lapdogs
woke up.

"What time is it?" snarled Snarler
McMurtagh.

"I was having a wonderful dream about
squirrels," yawned Butch Hilburg.

"What's that terrible smell?" asked The
Sundance Pup.

"Umph! Umph! Umph!" said Clive the
cockatoo.

The doorbell rang again.

Mr. Munroe climbed the stairs and opened
the door.

Four ladies came in. They looked strangely familiar.

Mr. Munroe presented each of them with their stolen jewels.

"Time to come home, you naughty, naughty boy," said Mrs. Armstrong.

The Sundance Pup wagged his tail.

"Walkies!" said Mrs. Lloyd.

Rupe the Fang barked excitedly.

"Here, boy!" said Mrs. Wilson, and Butch Hilburg rushed up to her.

"Come to Mummy!" cooed Pinky Neugerbauer. "My little poodle-doodle!"

"You'll never take me alive!" snarled Snarler McMurtagh.

The ladies thanked Mr. Munroe
for all his help. They promised
not to press charges as long as
the lapdogs behaved
themselves.

When they had gone, Mr. Munroe locked the
door of the old warehouse.

Then he picked up Clive the cockatoo and
set off toward the Pepperpot Building.

Chapter Ten

The Yellow Cat climbed in through the window of apartment 243 and looked around.

With one gloved paw, she reached into her bag and took out Mr. Munroe's drawing. She examined it carefully, then crept on tiptoe toward Ottoline's bedroom.

pening the door a crack, the Yellow Cat
pped inside. She didn't make a sound.

157

hen she sneaked over to the closet and
owly opened it. . . .

159

OTTOLINE'S NOTEBOOK

Suddenly a light flicked on.

With a startled meow the Yellow Cat sprang to her feet and dashed for the door.

Dodging a collapsing tower of neatly folded nightgowns . . .

ducking an avalanche of perfectly plumped pillows . . .

. . . she leaped over the vacuum cleaner and
the floor mop . . .

. . . and swerved under the swishing shower
curtain.

The Yellow Cat struggled to get a grip on the
shiny doorknob. She was about to try for
the window when . . .

. . . half a dozen home-cooked custard pies
sailed through the air toward her . . .

162

. . . and an incredibly large bear jumped out of the neatly made bed.

"Mrs. Jansen-Smith!" yowled the Yellow Cat.

163

The bear caught her in a big bear hug.
"Curses!" hissed the Yellow Cat.

164

"Hello," said Ottoline. "You didn't really think you'd get away with it, did you?"

"Tell me, how did you do it?" asked the Yellow Cat.

"Simple – with the help of my friends," said Ottoline, "and a clever plan."

OTTOLINE'S MADAGASCAN MOHAIR DRESSING GOWN →

165

Just then the doorbell rang.

It was Mr. Munroe and the pet police.

"We'll take it from here, miss," said the
pet policeman to Ottoline. "We've been
after these two for quite a while."

"What will happen to them?" asked
Ottoline.

"They'll be going away for a very long
time," said the policeman. "To a petting zoo
in the country."

"Curses!" said Clive the cockatoo.

Ottoline turned to Mr. Munroe and gave him a hug. "I'm very, very proud of you," she said.

Mr. Munroe nodded and Ottoline, who knew Mr. Munroe better than anyone else in the world, was sure that he was smiling.

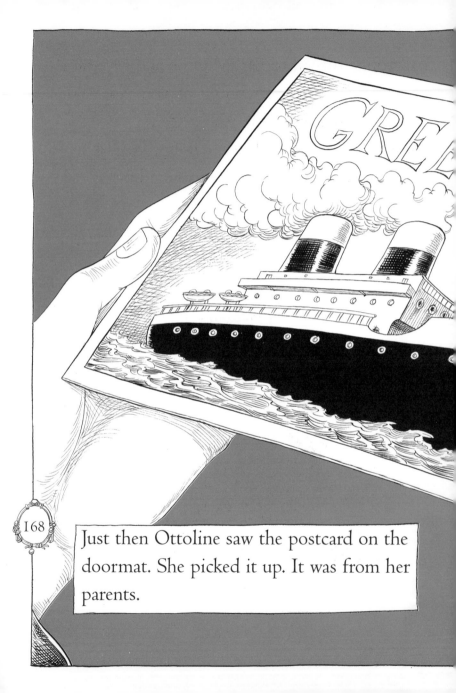

Just then Ottoline saw the postcard on the doormat. She picked it up. It was from her parents.

Dearest O,

'we are on our way home. Pa and I can't wait to see you,

lots of love,

Ma

P.S. Tell that nice bear he can stay as long as he wants.

P.P.S. Please clear up those custardpies, there's a good girl! XXX

Miss O. Brown,

Apartment 243,

The Pepperpot Bld.

3rd Street,

BIG CITY 3001

ACADEMY OF SUBTERFUGE

THIS IS TO CERTIFY THAT

Mr. Monroe

IS A CERTIFIED MASTER OF
DISGUISE

PROFESSOR MYSTERY
M.D.

Library of Congress Control Number: 2007934947
ISBN 978-0-06-144879-9 (trade bdg.) — ISBN 978-0-06-144880-5 (lib. bdg.)

1 2 3 4 5 6 7 8 9 10
❖
First American Edition, 2008
Originally published in Great Britain in 2007 by Macmillan Children's Books

Chris Riddell

1. Lives by the seaside in Brighton with his wife and three children.

2. Writes and illustrates books like these by himself, and books like these with Paul Stewart.

The Emperor of Absurdia

Ottoline and the Yellow Cat

THE BLOBHEADS

MUDDLE EARTH

THE EDGE CHRONICLES

THE FAR-FLUNG ADVENTURES

3. Draws a cartoon every Sunday for the Observer newspaper.

4. Has two of these in a box where he keeps his treasures →

KATE GREENAWAY MEDAL

KATE GREENAWAY MEDAL

and one each of these on his → son Jack's bookshelf.

SMARTIES GOLD AWARD

NESTLÉ SILVER AWARD

5. His favorite sweets are winegums. → They are the reason he became an illustrator.

FAIR

noes here.

tummy

1000-STRONG
LIGHT BULB

6c

CANADA

PEPPER POT PENCILS INC.

HB

HOME-COOKED
MEAL Co.

MENU

WAFFLE

PORRIDGE ☑

LATE ☑

A. TISH
SHOES LTD

BLESS YO

one pair of